This Walker book
belongs to:

_____

_____

To Jake and Ben and Wieland, dragon aces all – R. H.

First published 1980
by Jonathan Cape Ltd

Published 2015 by Walker Books Ltd
87 Vauxhall Walk, London SE11 5HJ

This edition published 2016

2 4 6 8 10 9 7 5 3 1

Text © 1980 the Estate of Russell Hoban • Illustrations © 1980, 2015 Quentin Blake

The right of Russell Hoban and Quentin Blake to be identified as author
and illustrator respectively of this work has been asserted by them in
accordance with the Copyright, Designs and Patents Act 1988

This book has been typeset in Goudy Old Style

Printed in China

British Library Cataloguing in Publication Data:
a catalogue record for this book is available from the British Library

ISBN 978-1-4063-4384-7

www.walker.co.uk

ACE DRAGON LTD

Russell Hoban
& Quentin Blake

WALKER BOOKS
AND SUBSIDIARIES
LONDON · BOSTON · SYDNEY · AUCKLAND

John was walking down the street when he heard something go Klonk.

John looked down and saw a round iron plate
in the pavement. It was like a manhole cover.
On it he read: ACE DRAGON LTD. John
stamped three times on the iron cover.

A voice said, "Who is it?"

John said, "John."

The voice said, "What do you want?"

John said, "I want to know what LTD means."

The voice said, "It means limited."

John said, "What does limited mean?"

The voice said, "It means I can't do everything. I can only do some things."

John said, "What can you do?"

The voice said, "I can make fire come out of my nose and mouth. I can fly. I can spin gold into straw if you have any gold."

John said, "I don't have any gold."

The voice said, "Do you need any straw?"

John said, "No."

The voice said, "Then it doesn't matter. Do you want to go flying with me?"

John said, "Yes, I do."

The voice said, "Then you have to come down and fight me. If you win, I'll take you flying."

John said, "I can't lift this iron cover.
It's too heavy. Can you lift it?"

The voice said, "No, I can't."

John said, "How can we meet, then?"

The voice said, "Take the Underground to
Dragonham East. I'll meet you there."

John said, "How shall I know you?"

The voice said, "I'll be wearing two pairs
of wellingtons. How shall I know you?"

John said, "I'll have a sword."

The voice said, "See you, then."

John said, "See you."

John took the Underground to Dragonham
East. There he saw a dragon in wellingtons.

The ace dragon said, "How do you do?
I'm Ace Dragon Ltd."
John said, "How do you do? I'm John."

Ace and John found some waste ground and got ready to fight.

Ace said, "Best out of three?"
John said, "Right."

Ace and John had their first fight.

John won.

Ace and John had their second fight.

John won.

John said, "That's two in a row.

That's best out of three. Now you have to take me flying."

John got on Ace's back and off they flew.

Ace and John flew very high and very far.
John said to Ace, "Can you do stunts? Can
you do sky-writing with fire?"

Ace did stunts and sky-writing with fire.

They were very high up and it was getting dark when Ace said, "I'm running out of petrol."

John said, "I didn't know you ran on petrol."

Ace said, "That's how I make my fire and that's what makes me go. I've used up so much petrol with the sky-writing that we haven't got enough to get us back."

John said, "Can't we glide back down to earth?"

Ace said, "No, we can't. If I stop flapping my wings we'll crash, and it's a very long way down."

John said, "Look! There's a little golden moon
below us. Can you get that far?"
Ace said, "I'll try."

They landed on the moon just as Ace ran out of petrol.

John said, "We could jump back down to earth if we had something soft to land on."

Ace said, "Yes, but we don't have something soft to land on."

John said, "This is a golden moon."
He sliced off some gold with his sword.
John said to Ace, "If you can spin gold
into straw you can make something soft for
us to land on."

Ace spun the gold into straw, then John sliced
off more gold and Ace spun more into straw.

Ace and John made a
great big bundle of straw.

Then they held on to the bundle as they jumped.

Thump! They landed safely in
the middle of the waste ground.

Ace said, "I have to go home for supper now."
John said, "So do I. You know what, Ace?"
Ace said, "What?"
John said, "You're not so limited."

Ace said, "Thanks. I'll see you."
John said, "See you."

Then they both
went home for
supper.

Other books
by Russell and Quentin:

ISBN 978-1-4063-6225-1

ISBN 978-1-4063-4382-3

ISBN 978-1-4063-4514-8

ISBN 978-1-4063-4381-6

ISBN 978-1-4063-4952-8

ISBN 978-1-4063-5564-2

ISBN 978-1-4063-4385-4

Available from all good booksellers

www.walker.co.uk